The Magical Mystery

by Ron Fogel

Illustrated by Marina Saumell

The Magical Mystery Pond
Copyright 2021 Ron Fogel

Published by Malissa Fogel
Printed in the United States of America.

Illustrated by Marina Saumell

ISBN: 978-1-7359404-0-3

Dedicated to Megan and Brian,
the inspiration for my imagination!

Once upon a time, a long time ago on the great plains of Africa on a bright sunny day a herd of white Horses came upon a strange pond among the trees. None of the horses could remember this pond being there before but they were all thirsty after being in the hot sun all day long.

They drank the water eagerly and the next day,
an amazing thing happened…

they all awoke with black stripes all over
their bodies, including their legs and heads.
They had become Zebras!
They were giddy with their new look!

The other animals were very curious, but the Hyenas were the most curious and they followed the Zebras the next day to the pond.

After the Zebras had left, the Hyenas snuck down to the pond and drank the sweet water.

The next day, they awoke with funny looking
spots all over their bodies.
This made them laugh and laugh and laugh!

The Giraffes, being so tall and able to see great distances, saw the funny looking stripes and spots on the Zebras and Hyenas. They seemed bored with the change, but they too were very thirsty in the hot sun as it had not rained for weeks.

As the Giraffes went to the trees to eat green leaves, they saw the mysterious new pond and quickly went over to drink. The Cheetahs were also very thirsty after a long day of running and chasing gazelle on the plains.

The Cheetahs saw the Giraffes by the trees and then joined them in drinking from the pond.

The next day, both the Giraffes and
Cheetahs awoke with spots on their hides.
Something magical was happening!

Over the next couple days, a few other animals made their
way to the mysterious pond to drink the water.
They awoke with various arrangements of stripes and spots.

None of the animals could understand what was happening
or why some animals got spots while others got stripes,
but they enjoyed their new look! It was truly magical
and mysterious!

Bongo

Leopard Tortoise

Pearl
Spotted Owl

Okapi

Guinea
Fowl

By the end of the week, the Lions finally saw the changes to the other animals. They were busy sleeping during the previous days and never bothered to find the "magical pond" that the other animals were talking about.

When the Lions finally made their way over to the trees to find the pond, the pond was nowhere to be found. They waited for two days, but the pond just disappeared and never returned!

Because of the Lions' laziness, they never got any spots or stripes…this made them very angry. This made them **ROAR** with displeasure!

When the magic pond disappeared in Africa, a similar pond mysteriously appeared in the jungles of Asia. A pride of large cats was stealthily searching for prey in the jungle when they came upon this mysterious new pond of water.

They decided to drink and guess what happened…

yes, the next day they awoke with black and white stripes, and now they are called Tigers!

The Magical Pond reappeared in several places in Asia where the Giant Pandas, Spotted Deer and many snakes drank the water.

And one day, the Magical Mystery Pond appeared in
the forests of South America where the mighty Jaguar,
a cousin of the Tiger, was the first to drink the water.
Unlike the Tiger, though, the Jaguar developed
beautiful spots rather than stripes.

One day, the pond appeared in North America, where Skunks, Racoons and Dalmations were the first to drink and they miraculously developed spots and stripes!

After that, for several weeks, the magical pond would disappear in one place and reappear somewhere else in the world, helping to create stripes and spots for animals all over the world.

Raccoons

North America

Badgers

Lynxes

South America

Jaguar

Many other animals drank the water until one day it disappeared
and never reappeared anywhere.

Maybe somewhere, some small boys and girls discovered
the pond and ended up with freckles!

Maybe the Magical Mystery Pond was a creation of God!

THE END

CPSIA information can be obtained
at www.ICGtesting.com
Printed in the USA
BVHW021318190421
605293BV00003B/53